Superlative Dawn

An Inner Adventure Romance

By Deni Rodgers

Dedicated to my, still now,
most present, and
highest teacher,

PR.

You told me if I wrote
I should
make it fiction at first . . . . so,
here is another story.

And to my father, who wanted
me to be a writer.

May we let imagination and science
meet inner experience.

TABLE OF CONTENTS

Chapter One: The Vessel

The *Superlative* cut through the Pacific waters at dawn, like a whisper through silk, her sleek white hull betraying nothing of the extraordinary cargo she carried. It was on a mission to change humanity. To any passing vessel—and there were few this far from the shipping lanes—she appeared to be just another research ship, perhaps studying marine life or ocean currents. Monstrously huge, yet not unlike a cruise ship, no one would guess that within her climate-controlled laboratories, rabbits floated in specially designed chambers, their long ears drifting upward in zero gravity, while white mice spun lazy spirals through the air, their tiny hearts monitored by sensors no larger than grains of rice.

Montana Reeves stood in the observation corridor of Lab Three, her bare feet silent on the rubberized flooring, watching a small Chocolate Dutch rabbit named Galileo tumble gently through his transparent enclosure. It was 4:47 in the morning—she'd checked the digital clock in the hallway—and the ship was at its quietest, the hum of the engines a low vibration she could feel in her bones. She preferred these hours, before the day shift arrived with their heavy footsteps and louder orders and the veterinary staff descended with their clipboards and concerned expressions.

In the dim blue light of the lab, Galileo's eyes caught hers. She pressed her palm against the acrylic wall of his chamber, and though she knew it was impossible, though she'd been told a hundred times by the scientists that anthropomorphizing the test subjects was unprofessional, she could have sworn the rabbit understood. His nose twitched twice—a greeting, she'd decided weeks ago— and then he pushed off from one wall with his powerful hind legs, sailing across the chamber in a graceful arc that would have been impossible on Earth; until now. A study of weightlessness and consciousness simultaneously.

"Good morning, sweet one," she whispered. Her voice, even at a whisper, seemed too loud in the sacred silence of pre-dawn. "How are you feeling today?"

2

The rabbit, of course, didn't answer. But Montana had learned to read the animals in other ways. The tilt of an ear. The brightness of an eye. The way they moved—or didn't move—through their weightless worlds. Galileo was thriving. She could see it in the glossy sheen of his coat, in the curious way he explored every corner of his enclosure, in when she'd hand-fed him fresh kale and carrot tops.

Not all of them were so fortunate. Work was needed.

Montana moved down the corridor, her loose cotton pants whispering against her legs, her tank top damp with the humidity, the ship's climate control could never quite eliminate. She'd tied her ash blonde hair back in a simple braid, though strands had already escaped to frame her face. At twenty-seven, she'd stopped worrying about such things. Stopped worrying. About a lot of things actually. Her yoga practice had taught her that.

3

In Chamber Seven, a white mouse named Valentina floated near the food dispenser, her pink nose working overtime. Montana smiled. Valentina was a survivor, a fighter. She'd been one of the first subjects in the zero-gravity trials, and unlike some of the others who'd grown disoriented or lethargic, Valentina had adapted almost immediately. She'd learned to navigate her three-dimensional world with the precision of a tiny astronaut, pushing off walls, catching herself mid-flight, even sleeping while anchored to the soft mesh netting Montana had installed in one corner.

Montana murmured, making a note on her tablet. "You're going to be famous."

Though of course, Valentina would never be famous. None of them would. The *Superlative* didn't exist, not officially. The work they were doing here—testing the long-term effects of weightlessness on living creatures, studying their adaptation, their breeding patterns, their survival rates—was classified at top secret level. Besides rabbits only live 10 years and it could take much longer to perfect weightlessness technology. Yet Valentina "two-point-zero" might go to ` Mars.

Montana had signed so many non-disclosure agreements when she'd taken this job that she'd lost count. She'd been fingerprinted, background-checked, interviewed by men in dark suits who'd asked her questions about her loyalty, her discretion, why she was married only for one year at age 23, and her ability to keep secrets.

She'd almost laughed at that last one. She'd been keeping secrets her whole life. Her father's military Top Secret Security Clearance was a discipline required of the entire family.

The ship rolled slightly, responding to a swell, and Montana felt it in her inner ear, notice. But she noticed everything now. Her practice of yoga had opened her up, stripped away the protective layers most people wore like armor. Sound was sharper. Light was brighter. Touch was almost unbearably intense. She'd learned to wear soft fabrics, to avoid fluorescent lights, when possible, not to burp at shocking pink, and to move through the world with a heightened awareness that was both a gift and a curse.

She continued her rounds, checking on each animal, making notes, adjusting food and water levels. There were twenty-three subjects currently in the zero-gravity chambers: twelve rabbits, eight mice, two guinea pigs, and one small tortoise named Armstrong who seemed utterly unbothered by the absence of gravity. The tortoise, Montana had decided, was either enlightened or completely oblivious. Possibly both.

In the regular-gravity holding area—the control group—another thirty animals waited their turn. Montana spent time with them too, though it broke her heart a little. They didn't know what was coming. They didn't know that soon they'd be floating, disoriented, in a world where up and down had no meaning.

But they'd adapt. Most of them would adapt. footsteps in the corridor—too early for the day shift, too heavy for Dr. Chen. Montana didn't turn around. She'd learned to identify people by their footsteps, their breathing, by the particular quality of energy they carried with them.

"You're up early." The voice was male, deep, with the faint trace of an accent she'd never been able to place. Russian, maybe. Or Ukrainian.

"I'm always up early, Dmitri," Montana said, still focused on the water bottles. "You know that."

Dmitri Volkov was the ship's chief engineer, a bear of a man with kind eyes and hands that could fix anything. He'd been one of the first people to speak to her when she'd boarded the *Superlative* six months ago, one of the few who didn't seem to find her silence off-putting or her bare feet unprofessional.

"The animals sleep better when you're here," he said, moving to stand beside her. "I've noticed."

Montana glanced at him, surprised. "That's not scientifically possible."

"Maybe not." He shrugged his massive shoulders. "But I notice things too." They stood in comfortable silence for a moment, Outside the porthole, the sky was beginning to lighten, deep purple fading to indigo.

"Do you ever think about what we're doing here?" Montana asked quietly. "Really doing?"

Dmitri was quiet for a long moment. "We're preparing for the future," he said finally. "Mr. Castellan believes humans will colonize Mars within twenty years. These animals—they're pioneers. Like the dogs the Soviets sent into space."

Montana thought of Laika, the Russian dog who'd died in orbit, alone and afraid. She pushed the thought away.

"And the secrecy?" she asked. "Why does it have to be secret?"

Dmitri's expression darkened. "You know why. After Nine Eleven, just five years ago—" He stopped, shook his head. "The world is different now. Dangerous. If people knew about this ship, about what we're doing, about the money Mr. Castellan has invested... There are those who would call it frivolous. Wasteful. There are those who would shut us down."

Montana understood. She'd been in New York City that day. . . had watched the towers fall. She had seen from a rooftop in Brooklyn, had felt the collective scream of a city, a nation, a world. The meditation had made her sensitive to such things—too sensitive. She'd felt the terror, the grief, the rage as if it were her own. For weeks afterward, she'd barely been able to function.

The *Superlative* had been her escape. A chance to disappear into the ocean, into work that mattered, into the simple routine of caring for creatures who asked nothing of her but food and water and gentle hands. Even cell-phone usage was not allowed anywhere within ½ mile of their experiments. She loved that.

"I should finish my rounds," Montana said, though she made no move to leave.

"And I should check the stabilizers," Dmitri replied, also not moving.

They stood together in the blue light, watching the animals float and drift, preparing for a future neither of them could quite imagine. Outside, the sun broke over the horizon, painting the Pacific in shades of gold and rose. The *Superlative* sailed on, carrying her secrets, carrying her cargo of dreamers and pioneers—human and animal alike—toward a destiny that felt both inevitable and impossible.

Montana pressed her hand against Galileo's chamber one more time, feeling the cool acrylic beneath her palm, feeling the subtle vibration of the ship's engines, feeling the above. She closed her eyes and breathed, centering herself, finding that still point within that the meditation had taught her to access.

In that moment of stillness, an image flashed through her mind: a red planet, a dome of glass, a rabbit hopping across rust-colored sand. She didn't know if it was vision or imagination, prophecy or wishful thinking. The collective unconscious spoke in symbols, in fragments, in possibilities rather than certainties.

She opened her eyes. Galileo was watching her, his nose twitching. It reminded her of how much energy goes into life with gravity. She was imagining a gymnasium in space, and then suddenly remembered she couldn't really appreciate a fitness room even at the best of hotels.

"Maybe," she whispered to him. "Maybe you will make it to Mars after all."

The rabbit pushed off from the wall and somersaulted through the air, and Montana could have sworn—though she knew it was impossible—that he was smiling.

Chapter Two: The Awakening

The meditation room occupied the entire starboard side of Deck Seven, a space that had once been designated for additional laboratories before Mr. Castellan had insisted on its conversion. "The mind is the greatest laboratory," he'd told the architects, and no one had dared argue. Now, floor-to-ceiling windows offered an unobstructed view of the endless Pacific, while the interior walls were painted in soft gradients of lavender and cream. A gong was beside the door and Tibetan singing bowls lined a mahogany shelf, and the air carried the faint scent of sandalwood.

Montana arrived early for the afternoon session; her notebook tucked under one arm. She'd spent the morning in the stables, and though she'd showered and changed into a simple linen floor-length dress the color of cranberries, she imagined she could still smell hay and horse on her skin. The room was empty except for one man sitting cross-legged near the stack of cushions, his back perfectly straight, his hands resting on his knees in a mudra she didn't recognize. something shifted in the air between them— a recognition that went beyond the physical, as though their souls had brushed against each other in passing.

"You must be Montana," he said, rising with fluid grace. He was tall and lean, dressed in light blue linen pants and a flowing beige shirt that somehow looked both casual and elegant. His dark shaped hair fell just past his defined shoulders, and his eyes were the deep brown of rich earth. "I'm Martin Crawls."

"The singer," Montana said, feeling suddenly awkward in the presence of such effortless charisma.

His smile was warm, self-deprecating. "Among other things. Though I know what you're thinking—what kind of name is Crawls for someone who's supposed to soar?" He'd clearly made this joke a thousand times, smoothing over the awkwardness that his unusual surname created. "My grandfather changed it from Crawlewski when he came

14

through Ellis Island. The immigration officer had terrible handwriting."

Montana found herself smiling back. There was something immediately disarming about him, a spiritual quality that seemed to emanate from his very being. She'd heard album had gone platinum three times over, songs about transcendence and human connection that had struck a chord with millions. He sang overtones like no other. But standing here, she understood that his appeal went deeper than his voice. He radiated a kind of light.

"Mr. Castellan invited me to observe the project," Martin continued, gesturing toward the meditation cushions arranged in a circle. "He thinks I might be able to help with the program. Apparently, I have some natural aptitude." He said this without arrogance, merely stating a fact.

"Have you worked with horses?" Montana asked.

"No, but I've worked with audiences of fifty thousand people," Martin said, his eyes twinkling. "Reading the energy of a crowd, knowing when to push forward and when to pull back, sensing what they need before they know it themselves. Mr. Castellan thinks it's the same principle. Connection without words. Understanding without explanation."

Before Montana could respond, the door opened, and other participants began filing in. She recognized several crew members, including Mitch, who entered with a large like a living stole. The cat's green eyes surveyed the room with regal indifference.

"That's Ptolemy," Mitch said, catching Montana's glance. He adjusted his thick glasses with his free hand. "He goes everywhere with me. Well, everywhere except the galley—health codes and all that. His brother Copernicus prefers to stay in the cabin. He's more of an introvert."

Mitch was perhaps thirty, with sandy hair that never quite lay flat and a face that

16

radiated kindness. His clothes were simple—khaki pants and a pressed white shirt—but impeccably clean. There was something endearing about the way he cradled the cat, as though it were the most natural thing in the world to bring a pet to meditation.

"Does he meditate with you?" Montana asked.

"In his own way," Mitch replied seriously. "Cats are naturally enlightened, I think. They don't need to work at it like we do."

The session leader arrived—a serene gentleman named Dr. Quynh Nguyen, who had studied with meditation masters in Kyoto, Dharamsala, and Hawaii. She smiled at the assembled group, her gaze lingering on Martin with obvious recognition, then settling on Montana with interest.

cushions or chairs. Today we'll be working on extending our awareness beyond the boundaries of self, by filling the body with sensation. We will start with a simple canon from limb to limb." Dr. Nguyen's voice was

17

soft but carried easily through the room. "Some of you have been practicing for weeks. Others are new. A guided sitting together allows us to exchange what some call the hydrogens of the higher self."

Montana settled onto a cushion between Martin and a woman from the marine biology team. She closed her eyes as instructed, focusing on her breath, trying to quiet the constant chatter of her mind. Dr. Nguyen's voice guided them through the initial stages—grounding, centering, opening by following the breath.

"Now," Dr. Nguyen said, "reach out with your awareness. Not with your hands, not with your eyes, but with that deeper sense that exists beyond the physical. Feel the presence of those around you. Notice the quality of their energy, the texture of their consciousness. Listen with your sensation."

Montana felt foolish at first, sitting there with her eyes closed, trying to sense something that might not even exist. But gradually, as her breathing deepened and her mind quieted, she became aware of something. It realizing you could perceive the shapes of furniture, the presence of walls, not by seeing them but by feeling the way they displaced the air.

To her left, Martin's presence felt like warm sunlight, golden and expansive. To her right, the marine biologist was a cool blue, focused and analytical. And Mitch, sitting across the circle with Ptolemy purring in his lap, was a soft green—steady, loyal, uncomplicated in the best possible way. The entirety of the room had a character . . . a hum . . .

Montana's eyes flew open in shock. She could feel them. Actually, feel them.

Martin was watching her, a knowing smile on his lips. He'd kept his eyes open throughout, she realized. He nodded slightly, as if to say: Hello, fellow seeker of self-knowledge.

The session continued for another thirty minutes, yet Montana attention floated in

19

and out. Her heart was racing with the implications of what she'd experienced. If she could sense human consciousness, could she truly connect with the horses in the same way? Was this the key to everything Mr. Castellan had envisioned? She let go of her inner dialogue and allowed her heart, mind, and body to be present.

bowl to signal the end of the session, Montana felt both exhilarated and exhausted. The other participants filed out slowly, some chatting quietly, others maintaining the meditative silence. Mitch paused to scratch Ptolemy behind the ears, whispering something to the cat before heading toward the door.

"Your first breakthrough," Martin said, standing beside her. "I could feel it happen. Like a light switching on."

"Is it always like that for you?" Montana asked.

"It's different for everyone. For me, it's like hearing music that no one else can hear—the

20

symphony of human emotion and intention."
He tilted his head, studying her. "For you, I
think it will be more tactile. You'll feel your
way through it. It suits you."

Before Montana could ask what he meant,
the door opened again, and two men
entered. The first was Mr. Castellan himself,
his attendance immediately commanding
attention. He was perhaps fifty, with silver
threading through his dark hair and eyes
that burned with fierce intelligence and
ambition. He wore jeans and a black
turtleneck, the uniform of visionary
entrepreneurs, and moved with the coiled
night and considered it to be too much.

The second man was younger, perhaps forty,
with the build of someone who'd spent time
in military service. His hair was sandy, wavy
and parted dramatically on the side, and his
eyes—a striking pale blue—swept the room
with tactical precision before settling on
Montana. He wore cargo pants and a fitted
black t-shirt that revealed muscular arms

marked with scars that looked like they had stories behind them.

"Ah, Montana," Mr. Castellan said, his face lighting up. "Martin. Perfect. I wanted to introduce you both to Mark Rubin. Mark built this ship—every bolt, every weld, every system. He's staying aboard to ensure our work isn't compromised by those who would steal what we're creating here."

Mark extended his hand, first to Martin, then to Montana. His grip was firm, his palm calloused. "Ms. Reeves," he said, his British accent crisp and precise. "I've heard about your work with the horses. Impressive results in a short time."

There was something intense about Mark Rubin, an edge that made Montana think of a blade kept perpetually sharp. He looked at the ship the way she looked at horses—with beyond professional pride.

"The ship is more than steel and technology," Mark continued, his gaze returning to Montana with unsettling focus.

"She's a living thing, in her way. She needs to be understood, respected, protected. Not everyone grasps that."

"Mark takes his responsibilities seriously," Mr. Castellan said with a slight smile. "Sometimes I think he loves this ship more than anything else in the world."

"Someone has to," Mark replied without humor. "There are governments, corporations, individuals who would kill to possess what we're developing here. The weightlessness research, not to be compared to anti-gravity, alone is worth billions. The applications for military intelligence, corporate espionage, diplomatic negotiations—" He stopped himself, as if remembering he was speaking to civilians.

"Let's just say I don't sleep much."

"Speaking of the research," Mr. Castellan said, turning to Montana, "I'd like you to observe the weightlessness experiments tomorrow. We have the B-29 on Deck Twelve—we've converted it into a testing environment like a KC-135. We're working with smaller animals first, trying for consciousness, their ability to connect. And we have the water tanks on Deck Nine for similar work. I think you'll find it fascinating."

Montana nodded, though her mind was reeling. A B29 aircraft, on a ship? Water tanks for weightlessness? The scope of Mr. Castellan's vision was staggering, despite the alphabet soup of equipment.

"The goal," Mr. Castellan continued, his eyes blazing with passion, "is to understand consciousness itself. To map it, enhance it, transmit it. We believe consciousness is accentuated by sensory deprivation or weightlessness. The kind of weightlessness that one would experience in inter-planetary travel. Imagine a world where distance is no barrier to connection, where understanding flows as easily as conversation, where the barriers between minds dissolve. That's what we're building here. That's what you're all part of."

Martin was nodding slowly, his expression thoughtful. "And the horses are the key?"

"They're one key," Mr. Castellan said. "Their consciousness is different from ours—less cluttered with logic and rationality, more direct. If we can bridge that gap, we can bridge any gap. Montana is proving that Montana, assessing. "Can you really read their minds?" he asked bluntly.

Montana considered the question carefully. "I don't think it's reading, exactly.

It's more like... feeling what they feel.

Knowing what they need.

Understanding their intentions before they act on them."

"And today?" Martin asked gently. "In the meditation?"

Montana felt heat rise to her cheeks. "Today I felt all of you in attendance. Just for a moment. But it was real."

Mr. Castellan's smile was triumphant. "You see, Mark? This is why I brought her here. Natural talent, combined with the right training, in the right environment. We're going to change the world."

As the men continued talking, discussing schedules and security protocols and research parameters, Montana found herself studying them. Mr. Castellan with his boundless vision and relentless drive. Martin with his spiritual grace and intuitive gifts. Mark with his fierce protectiveness and warrior's vigilance. And somewhere on this ship, Mitch with his cats and his gentle loyalty, content to participate without needing to excel.

this impossible project in the middle of the Pacific. And somehow, Montana was at the center of it, a horse whisperer who was learning to whisper to something far more complex than horses.

She thought of Stardust and her colt, Nebula, waiting in the stables below. She thought of the B-29 aircraft and the water tanks and all the mysteries this ship contained. And she thought of the feeling she'd had in meditation— that moment of connection, of truly touching another's consciousness.

Whatever was awakening inside her, Montana realized, was only the beginning.

The real journey was just starting to unfold.

Chapter Three: Weightless

The morning sun cast diamonds across the Pacific as Montana made her way to the forward deck, where the modified B-29 aircraft sat like a silver bird waiting to take flight. The ship had been designed with this very purpose in mind—a floating runway that could launch experimental aircraft into the sky, testing the boundaries of what was possible when gravity itself became negotiable.

"Careful there," Mark Rubin's voice came from behind her, that distinctly British accent wrapping around the words like velvet. "The deck's still wet from the morning wash."

Montana turned, her heart doing that peculiar flutter it had begun doing whenever Mark was near. He stood in the early light, his dark hair slightly tousled by the sea breeze, his eyes—those impossibly pale blue eyes—fixed on her with an intensity that made her breath catch.

"Thank you," she managed, acutely aware of how his accent transformed even the simplest words into something that seemed to resonate in her chest. There was

vowels, the crisp consonants, the slight roll of certain syllables that made her want to listen to him read the ship's technical manual just to hear him speak.

She's curious about me, Mark thought, a small smile playing at his lips. *The way she looks at me when I talk—*

Montana's eyes widened. She had heard that. Not with her ears, but somewhere deeper, in that place where her father's voice still echoed with warnings about men and their intentions. But this was different. This was Mark's actual thoughts, clear as if he'd spoken them aloud.

"Are you alright?" Mark asked, stepping closer. "You've gone quite pale."

"I'm fine," she said quickly, but her mind was reeling. The psychic abilities her father had always dismissed as "women's intuition" or "lucky guesses" were growing stronger. Out here on the open seas, away from the noise of civilization, something was awakening inside her.

Mark reached out, his hand hovering near her elbow, not quite touching but close enough that she could feel the warmth radiating from his skin. "Perhaps you should sit down. The sun can be quite intense, even this early, yes?." Before she could respond, hangar, his presence immediately commanding attention. Where Mark was all refined athletic elegance, Martin was raw intensity—broad-shouldered and confident, with eyes that seemed to see straight through to her soul.

She heard him, Martin's thought came to her as clearly as Mark's had, and Montana realized with a shock that Martin knew. He knew about her abilities because he shared them. Their eyes met across the deck, and in that moment, an understanding passed between them that needed no words.

"We're ready for the first test," Martin announced, his voice steady and professional, but Montana could feel the undercurrent of something else— concern, protectiveness, and something warmer that made her pulse quicken. "Montana, Mr. Castellan wanted you to observe. We're sending up Ramses and Newton today."

Ramses and Newton were two of the rhesus monkeys who had become unexpected companions during the voyage. Ramses was the smaller of the two, with intelligent eyes and a mischievous streak that had endeared him to the entire crew. Newton was larger, more serious, with a dignified bearing that seemed almost human in his reflective nature.

laboratory, learning their personalities, earning their trust. Ramses would steal pens from her pocket and try to draw on her notebooks. Newton would sit quietly, watching her work with an expression that suggested he understood far more than a monkey should.

"Are they ready?" she asked, pushing aside her confusion about the psychic connection with Martin to focus on the animals' welfare.

"Come see for yourself," Mark said, gesturing toward the hangar. As they walked, he stayed close enough that their shoulders nearly touched, and Montana found herself hyper-aware of every movement, every breath.

Inside the hangar, the B-29 had been transformed into a flying laboratory. The bomb bay had been converted into a pressurized chamber where the animals would experience brief periods of weightlessness as the aircraft executed parabolic arcs—climbing steeply, then diving, creating moments where gravity seemed to disappear. The aircraft had been nicknamed the "Vomit Comet".

Mitch Henderson was already there, making final adjustments to the monitoring

32

equipment. Unlike Mark's refined elegance or practical, grounded quality that Montana found oddly comforting. His hands were steady as he worked, his movements efficient and sure.

"All systems check out," Mitch reported, looking up with a smile that crinkled the corners of his eyes. "These little guys are going to be fine. I've triple checked every seal, every gauge. Your father taught me well."

There was something in the way he said it—a respect for her father, yes, but also a subtle acknowledgment of her own expertise. Mitch never talked down to her, never assumed she needed things explained twice. He treated her as an equal, and Montana appreciated that more than he probably knew. Especially since she was the daughter of his previous mentor, Hugh Reeves, principal contributor to weightlessness research.

"Ramses is excited," she observed, watching the smaller monkey bounce in his specially designed harness. "Newton seems more philosophical about the whole thing."

"Rather like their namesakes, I'd imagine," Mark said, that accent making even scientific observation sound like poetry. "One all contemplating the deeper implications."

Montana laughed, and the sound seemed to brighten the hangar. She caught Martin watching her, his expression unreadable but his thoughts—those thoughts she could now hear—full of warmth and something deeper, something that both thrilled and frightened her.

She has no idea how beautiful she is when she laughs, Martin thought, and Montana felt heat rise to her cheeks.

The test flight was both exhilarating and terrifying. Montana watched from the observation deck as the B-29 climbed into the brilliant blue sky, her heart in her throat despite knowing that every precaution had been taken. Through the radio link, she could hear the pilot's calm voice calling out altitude and trajectory, and then—

"Entering parabolic arc. Three... two... one... weightless."

On the video monitors, she watched Ramses and Newton float free of their perches, their expressions a mixture of confusion and wonder. Ramses immediately began doing somersaults in the air, chattering with what could only be described as delight. Newton moved more carefully, testing this new reality with cautious grace.

eyes on the medical monitors. "Heart rate elevated but within normal parameters. Respiration steady. They're handling it beautifully."

Montana felt tears cloud her eyes. This was what her father, from Air Force to NASA, had worked toward for so many years—proof that living beings could survive and even thrive in conditions that defied everything humans had known since the dawn of time.

"Thirty seconds of weightlessness," the pilot's voice crackled over the radio.

"Preparing to pull out."

As gravity reasserted itself, both monkeys returned smoothly to their perches, Ramses still chattering excitedly while Newton sat with that same dignified composure, as if floating in midair was simply another interesting experience to be catalogued and considered.

"Brilliant," Mark breathed, standing so close to Montana that she could feel the warmth of his body. "Absolutely brilliant.

Martin was on her other side, and she was acutely aware of being flanked by these two very different men, both of whom seemed to radiate an interest in her that went far beyond professional collaboration. Her father's warning echoed in her mind—*Men see your beauty, your intelligence, and they'll want to possess both. Be careful. Be very careful.*

36

But standing here, watching history being made, feeling the genuine excitement and respect from Mark and Martin and Mitch, Montana wondered if her father's warning had been born from his own fears from his personal past, rather than any real danger. These men didn't seem to want to possess her. They seemed to want to... know her. To understand her. To share this extraordinary moment with her.

You're safe with us, Martin's thought came to her, gentle and reassuring. *I promise you that.*

She turned to look at him, and their eyes met. In that moment, Montana understood that the psychic connection between them was both a gift yet also a responsibility. He could read her fears, her doubts, her growing attraction to all three of these

remarkable men. And somehow, that

vulnerability didn't feel dangerous. It felt like trust.

37

That afternoon, while the scientists analyzed data from the flight test,

Montana found herself in the water tank laboratory where other experiments were an entire section of the lower deck, filled with seawater and designed to simulate various underwater conditions, including weightlessness. When covered Montana would walk across the top just to test her own sense of balance and would sometimes meditate sitting cross-legged in the very center of the covered pool

Mitch was there, having just completed a dive to repair one of the underwater cameras. He emerged from the tank like some mythical sea creature, water streaming from his wetsuit, his hair plastered to his head. He scrambled for his glasses after removing his goggles. He saw Montana and grinned, that easy, uncomplicated smile that made her feel like she could breathe freely.

"Want to see something amazing?" he asked, stripping off his diving gloves.

38

"Always," she replied.

He led her to a smaller observation tank where several dolphins circled gracefully. "We've been teaching them to retrieve objects from different depths," Mitch explained. "But watch this—this is something they figured out on their own."

He dropped a small ball into the tank, and immediately the dolphins began playing an elaborate game, passing the ball between seemed almost choreographed. But more than that, they were clearly communicating—clicks and whistles that had meaning, purpose.

"They're talking to each other," Montana whispered, enchanted.

"More than that," Mitch said softly. "They're creating. That's not just communication—that's art. That's joy."

Montana looked at him with new appreciation. Beneath the practical, healthy exterior was a man who understood beauty, who recognized the profound in the everyday. He caught her

39

looking and held her gaze, and for a moment, the air between them seemed charged with possibility.

"Mitch, I—" she began, but was interrupted by the ship's alarm—three short blasts that meant all hands to stations.

They ran to the deck together, where 1st Captain Morrison was already barking orders. On the horizon, dark clouds were gathering with unnatural speed, and the sea that had been calm all morning was beginning to churn. "Storm coming in fast," the captain shouted over the rising wind. "Secure all equipment. Get those animals below deck. Move!"

As the crew scrambled to prepare, Montana felt something else—a prickling at the base of her skull, a sense of wrongness that had nothing to do with the weather. She looked out at the darkening horizon and sensed, with absolute certainty, that something was coming. Something more ominous than any storm.

Martin appeared at her side, his face grim. "You feel it too," he said. It wasn't a question.

"What is it?" she asked.

"I don't know," he admitted. "But whatever it is, it's been following us. And I think it's finally caught up."

The wind picked up, whipping Montana's hair across her face, and as the first drops of rain began to fall, she realized that their peaceful days of scientific discovery were over. The real test—whatever it might be—was about to begin.

And somewhere in the chaos of preparation, as Mark rushed past with equipment, as Mitch secured the aircraft, as Martin stood beside her watching the storm approach, Montana understood that her father's warning had been right about one thing: her life was about to change forever. Just not in the way he'd feared.

The men around her weren't a danger to avoid. They were allies she would need for whatever was coming. And the psychic

41

abilities she'd always hidden, always downplayed, were about to become the very thing that might save them all.

The storm hit with the force of a hammer, and the *Superlative* pitched into the darkness, carrying its precious cargo of dreamers and animals and secrets into the unknown.

Chapter Four: The Storm Within

The B-29 reappeared first as a shadow against the bruised sky, its engines screaming into the wind that had risen from nowhere. Montana stood at the rail, her hair whipping across her face, watching as the vintage bomber fought its way back toward the deck. The ocean had transformed in the hour since takeoff—what had been gentle swells now rolled in dark, muscular waves that lifted the converted carrier and dropped it with sickening irregularity.

"Holy God," Mitch muttered beside her, his knuckles white on the railing. "They're actually going to try to land in this." He threw his hands into the air and spun full circle, back to the rail.

The wind gusted to forty knots, maybe more. Montana could taste salt spray on her lips, felt the deck shifting beneath her feet like an angry dragon. With less than a quarter tank of gas remaining, the B-29 made its approach, too fast, the pilot fighting crosswinds that wanted to flip the massive aircraft like a toy. She held her breath as the wheels touched down, bounced, touched again. The screech of rubber on wet metal was sickening, belching above the storm's roar.

Then, after escorting the pilot to safety, Martin, as co-pilot, was climbing down from the cockpit, his flight suit brightly glistening with moisture, and their eyes met across thirty feet of heaving deck.

The connection hit her like a physical blow.

Montana gasped, her hand flying to the rail for support as sensation flooded through her body—not her own sensation, but *his*. She felt the adrenaline still coursing through his veins due to the landing, felt the way his heart hammered against his sternum, felt the electric awareness of her presence that made his skin hyper-sensitive and his breath catch. But more than that, she felt his *desire*, utterly raw, all-encompassing and overwhelming, a psychic touch that moved through her body like hands, like lips, like—

Her knees buckled slightly. Heat bloomed low in her belly, spreading outward in waves that made her gasp again. She was dimly aware of Mitch asking if she was all right, but she couldn't answer, couldn't speak, could only grip the railing as pleasure built inside her with shocking intensity. Martin hadn't moved, hadn't touched her, was still twenty feet away, but she felt him everywhere, felt live wire, pulsing and urgent and so powerful that her body responded as if he were actually—

"Montana?" Mitch's hand on her shoulder broke the spell.

She blinked, shuddering, and found she was trembling. Across the deck, Martin had turned away, his shoulders rigid with tension. She knew—*knew* with absolute certainty—that he had shared everything she had felt, that the connection flowed both ways, that he was as shaken as she was.

45

"I'm fine," she managed, though her voice came out breathless and unsteady. "Just... the storm. It's getting worse."

It was true. In the minutes since the B-29's landing, the sky had darkened to the color of a bruise, and the wind had risen to a howl. The first real rain came then, not a drizzle but a deluge, sheets of water that turned the deck into a treacherous skating rink. Lightning split the sky, close enough that Montana could smell ozone.

"Everyone below!" 2nd Captain Rodriguez's voice boomed over the PA system. "Secure all aircraft! This is not a drill!"

The next six hours were a nightmare of pitching decks and screaming wind. After wedged herself into her cabin, listening to the storm tear at the ship like a living thing. She heard crashes, shouts, the groan of metal under stress. Once, the ship rolled so far to starboard that books flew from her shelf and her laptop slid across the floor. She thought of Martin, wondered if he was afraid, and felt an echo of his presence in her mind—steady, calm, almost meditative despite the chaos.

When dawn finally came, gray and exhausted, Montana emerged to find the deck transformed. One of the smaller aircraft—a Cessna that had belonged to a collector from Portland—was simply gone, torn loose and swallowed by the sea. All the deck chairs . . . all the deep-sea fishing poles . . . gone. Debris littered every surface. And when she made her way to the bridge, she found Captain Rodriguez staring at instruments with an expression that made her stomach clench.

"How bad?" she asked.

He didn't sugarcoat it. "Navigation system's fried! Radio's intermittent at best. We're taking on water in two compartments—not enough to sink us, but enough to be a problem. And the storm pushed us at least two hundred miles off course." He paused, Reeves. And we're alone out here."

The meeting in the main hangar that afternoon had the feeling of a war council. Forty-seven people—all that remained of the original crew and passengers—gathered among the aircraft, their faces drawn with exhaustion and fear. Captain Rodriguez, laid out the situation with military precision: limited fuel, damaged systems, and most critically, food supplies that would last perhaps two weeks if they were careful.

"Two weeks?" Mark's voice cut through the murmurs. He stood near the front, his expensive casual wear rumpled but his presence still commanding. "That's unacceptable. We need to take action now."

"What kind of action?" Mitch asked. He was sitting on a crate near Montana, his practical engineer's mind already working through problems and solutions.

Mark gestured toward the makeshift pens where the animals were kept—the dogs, the cats, the monkeys, the exotic birds that various passengers had brought along as pets and the experimental "lab rats". "We have resources we're not utilizing. Those animals consume food and water we can't spare. If we're going to survive—"

48

"You want to throw people's pets and cultured experiment animals overboard?" Montana heard the horror in her own voice.

"I want us to *live*," Mark said flatly. "Sentiment is a luxury we can't afford. Every pound of animal food, every gallon of water that goes to a critter, is a pound and a gallon that could keep a human being alive, yes?"

"There are other options." Mitch stood, his voice wavering but firm. "I've been looking at the fishing equipment in storage. The ocean is full of food if we know how to get it. I can rig lines, teach people how to catch tuna, mahi-mahi. We are not cavemen here."

"Fishing?" Mark's laugh was sharp. "You want to bet our lives on your ability to catch enough fish to feed fifty people?"

"I want to try every option before we start over-boarding animals."

The argument escalated, voices rising, taking sides. Montana felt the tension in the room like a physical pressure, felt the fear beneath the anger. These were people who had boarded the ship expecting an adventure, a unique journey, a rewarding job, and now found themselves in a genuine survival challenge.

Then Martin spoke, his voice quiet but somehow cutting through the noise.

The hangar fell silent. Everyone turned to look at him. He stood slightly apart from the group, his expression serene despite the chaos around them. He did go flush for a moment, Montana observed, yet he inhaled, in order to continue . . .

"Meditate?" Mark's tone dripped with contempt. "We're drifting in the middle of the Pacific with two worth of food, no satellite contact or air traffic, and you want to meditate?"

"I want us to focus on our collective consciousness," Martin said calmly. "To send out a signal, a call for help. There are forces in the universe that respond to intention, to focused mental energy. If we all concentrate together, visualize rescue, project that

50

scenario of need and solution into the cosmos—"

"This is insane," Mark interrupted. "We need practical solutions, not 'New Age' nonsense."

"It's not nonsense." Martin's eyes found Montana's across the hangar, and she felt that connection again, gentler this time but still powerful. "Montana knows. She's felt it. The connection between minds, between consciousness and reality. We're not as powerless as we think."

Montana felt every eye turn to her. She thought about the psychic connection she'd experienced with Martin, the way she'd felt his presence in her mind, the intensity of their bond. Was it really so impossible that focused intention could affect reality? That purity of attention could reach out beyond the physical, through refinement of the spectrum of vibrations between light and matter?

But she also thought about Mitch's practical approach, his willingness to work with what they had. And even Mark's harsh pragmatism came from a place of wanting to survive, to protect human life.

"I think," she said slowly, "we need to try everything. Mitch's fishing. Conservation of resources. And yes, maybe Martin's meditation too. We can't afford to dismiss any possibility."

"Even if that possibility is killing the animals?" Mark pressed.

Montana met his eyes. "That should be our last resort. Not our first."

The meeting broke up without clear resolution, people drifting away in small groups, still arguing, still afraid. Montana found herself standing alone near the rail as afternoon faded toward evening. The storm had passed, but the ocean remained restless, and the sky held the promise of more weather to come.

She felt them before she saw them—three distinct presences approaching. Mitch from the left, carrying fishing line and hooks, his face set with determination. Mark from the right, his expression calculating as he studied the animal pens. And Martin from behind, his psychic presence a warm pressure against her mind and physical sensation.

Three men. Three approaches to survival. Three different futures pulling at her, demanding she choose.

Montana gripped the rail and stared out at the endless ocean, feeling the ship drift beneath her feet, feeling the weight of impossible decisions settling on her shoulders like the gathering dark.

The external storm had passed, but she knew with absolute certainty that the real internal tempest was only beginning.

Chapter Five: Entanglement

Time became endlessly fluid on the huge, yet limited, vessel, measured not in hours but in the arc of the sun across an endless sky, in the rhythm of waves that rocked them like a cradle that would not let them sleep. Three days became four, then five. The emergency rations dwindled. The water supply, carefully rationed, dropped to levels that made Mark's jaw tighten each time he checked the containers and eyed the pens.

But Mitch proved himself invaluable in ways none of them had anticipated, despite the fact that most of the fishing poles had washed overboard.

On the morning of the fourth day, he fashioned a fishing line from dental floss he'd found in the emergency kits, while bending a tent tarp grounding fastener into a crude hook. He used a scrap of the silver emergency blanket as a lure, and within an hour, he'd pulled up several small mahi-mahi, their scales flashing green and gold in the sunlight. Mark had looked at him with something approaching respect for the first time since the storm.

"Grew up fishing the Chesapeake with my grandfather," Mitch said simply, gutting the said the bay would provide if you knew how to ask. This will supplement our supplies. Obviously though we need to have everyone find their floss, etcetera."

Martin watched Montana's face as Mitch worked, saw the softness that entered her eyes. The fish was divided into portions, eaten raw because they had to save propane for heat. The taste was clean and sweet, and it felt like salvation.

By the fifth day, Mitch had caught twelve more fish. He'd also rigged a better sun shelter using pieces of the ship's auxiliary sail canopy, creating shade that made the midday heat bearable. He told stories in the evening—funny ones about his childhood, about his grandmother's church in Baltimore, about the time he'd accidentally joined a salsa dancing class thinking it was a cooking course. His laughter was genuine and infectious, and even Mark smiled despite himself.

Montana sketched Mitch one afternoon, her charcoal moving quickly across the nearly damp pages of her journal. She captured something essential in his face—a kindness that ran deeper than circumstance, a steadiness that didn't require recognition. stranger was happening.

Something that defied the ordinary physics of human connection.

If consciousness could be described in quantum terms—and Montana had read enough to know that some scientists believed it could—that what was occurring between her and Martin resembled nothing short of quantum entanglement. Two particles, once connected, remaining correlated across any distance, each one's state instantaneously affecting the other's, regardless of the space between them.

They had become entangled.

It started small. On the fourth day, they both reached for the water container at exactly the same moment, their hands colliding in the space above it. They laughed, pulled back, then reached again—simultaneously. Three times this happened before Martin finally grabbed it and handed it to her, something unreadable flickering in his dark eyes.

"Sorry," they said in unison, then stopped, staring at each other.

Later that afternoon, Montana was thinking about her studio in Brooklyn, about the painting she'd left unfinished on her easel—a swirling head of hair floating upward like seaweed. She was wondering if she'd ever see it again when Martin spoke.

"Do you paint?" he asked suddenly.

She turned to him, startled. "Yes. How did you—?!"

"I don't know," he said, looking equally surprised. "I just... I had this image in my mind. A woman underwater. Your work?"

The hair on her arms stood up despite the heat.

The next day, she was sitting at the edge of the ship, trailing her fingers in the water, when she felt Martin's presence behind her before he made a sound. She turned, and there he was, settling down beside her in the exact spot she'd somehow known he would occupy.

"I was just coming to sit here," he said.

"I know," she replied, and she did know. She had felt his intention like a ripple in still water, like the collapse of a wave function into a single, certain reality.

In quantum mechanics, particles existed in superposition—in multiple states simultaneously—until observed. The act of observation collapsed the wave function, when two observers became so entangled that they collapsed into the same state? When their wave functions merged?

Martin began leading meditation sessions in the evenings, as the sun descended toward the horizon and painted the sky in shades of amber and rose. He would sit cross-legged at the center of the ship's meditation hall, his voice low and steady, guiding them through breathing exercises, through body scans, through visualizations of safety and rescue.

"Notice the breath," he would say. "Notice how it comes and goes without effort. You are not separate from this ocean, from this sky. You are part of the same system, the same field of energy and awareness."

Mark participated reluctantly at first, but even he seemed to find some relief and meaning in the practice. Mitch took to it naturally, his face becoming peaceful, his responsible shoulders relaxing.

But for Montana, the meditations became something else entirely.

When Martin spoke, she could receive his words not just in her ears but in her body, as if they were vibrations tuning her to a frequency she'd always been capable of receiving but had never quite accessed. And when she closed her eyes and followed his physical presence a few feet away, but something deeper. His consciousness felt like a warmth beside her own, like two flames burning close enough to share the same air . . . the air that surrounds the earth and that the trees inhale and exhale with each rotation of the planet.

Once, during a meditation, she opened her eyes and found him already looking at her, his eyes open too, as if he'd felt the exact moment of her return to ordinary awareness. As if they were operating on the same clock, the same quantum rhythm.

"Did you feel that?" he whispered.

She nodded, unable to speak.

Quantum coherence, she thought. When quantum states maintain their relationship, their phase correlation, without collapsing into classical separateness. They were maintaining coherence.

But coherence was fragile. It required isolation from the environment, from decoherence, from the noise of the outside world. And there were 40 other people on this ship.

She watched Mitch as he checked his fishing line, his movements patient and sure. She watched Mark as he inventoried their supplies for the dozenth time, his face drawn with worry that was beginning to curdle into something harder.

The animals were suffering.

The dogs had stopped eating as the temperature went from cold at night to hot during the day. They lay in the shade of Mitch's shelter, panting, their eyes glazed. The cats were lethargic, barely moving. One of the rabbits had died on the fifth day, and Mark had slipped it overboard without ceremony, his face rigid.

"We need to reduce their water ration," Mark said on the sixth morning. "We're going through it too fast."

"They're already getting almost nothing," Montana protested.

"Then we give them nothing," Mark snapped. "We're not going to die so a bunch of animals can live a few more days."

"They're not just animals," she said, her voice rising. "They're—"

"They're cargo," Mark interrupted. "That's all they ever were. Cargo that's now a liability."

Martin placed a hand on Montana's arm, and the touch sent a current through her—not sexual, exactly, but electric, a transfer of intensified everything she was feeling.

"Let's not make any decisions when we're this stressed," Martin said calmly. "We're all dehydrated. We're all scared. Let's wait until evening, see how we feel then."

Mark glared at him but said nothing.

That afternoon, Montana painted. She'd been rationing her art supplies as carefully as they rationed water, but she needed to externalize what was happening inside her, needed to give it form.

She painted Martin.

Yet, not as he appeared on the ship. She painted him as she saw him in her mind's eye during their meditations—as a figure made of light, his form dissolving at the edges into waves, into particles, into pure energy. She painted herself beside him, equally luminous, their boundaries blurring where they met, their wave functions overlapping in a symmetrical prismatic Northern Light, Aurora Borealis, display.

She painted entanglement.

When Martin saw it, he went very still. He stared at the image for a long time, and when he finally looked up at her, his eyes been tears.

"You see it too," he said. It wasn't a question.

"I don't know what I'm seeing," she admitted. "But yes. I see something." That night, she had a vision, in her room.

She was lying on the ship, hovering in that space between waking and sleep, when suddenly she was somewhere else. She was underwater, deep underwater, and there was a light approaching from below. A massive shape, dark and cylindrical, rising through the blue depths like a whale, like a god.

A submarine.

She gasped and sat up, her heart pounding.

Martin was already sitting up too, staring at his cabin wall from across the ship. He bounded down the hall, trying to tip-toe yet gleefully skipping like a child. Her door was open when he got to her cabin.

"You saw it?" he said.

"How do you—?"

"Because I saw it too. Just now. A submarine."

where entangled particles share information instantaneously, regardless of distance. But they weren't distant. They were here, together, their consciousness somehow sharing the same space, the same visions.

"It's coming," Montana whispered. "I know it's coming."

"Yes," Martin agreed. "Soon."

Mitch, awakened by the skipping, was watching them with an expression of wonder and confusion. "What are you two talking about?"

But Mark was watching them with something else in his eyes. Something that looked like fear, or anger, or perhaps jealousy of a connection he couldn't access, couldn't understand.

"You're both losing it," he said flatly. "Heat stroke. Dehydration. There's no submarine."

But Montana knew better. She could feel it now, a certainty that had nothing to do with logic or hope. The submarine was real. It was coming.

65

And when it finally arrived, everything would change.

She looked at Martin; at Mitch; at Mark. Three men, three possible futures, three wave functions that hadn't yet collapsed into a single reality. Her heart was a quantum system, existing in superposition, in multiple states at once. She could see the active in Martin, the passive in Mitch, and the neutralizing in Mark.

She loved Martin's depth, his spiritual intensity, the way their souls seemed to recognize each other across some vast distance.

She loved Mitch's kindness, his steadiness, the way he made her feel safe and cared for without asking for anything in return.

And Mark—Mark she tried to love for his extremely handsome ruggedness, and she understood his fear, his desperation to survive. She saw the man he might have been under different circumstances and his commitment to finding the next solution.

She saw their relationships as evolving in and out of each other's intentions and events. How did she fit in? They were interacting with each other and keeping the experiment in consciousness evolving.

The observer effect, she thought. In quantum mechanics, the act of observation changes what is observed. But what if she was both observer and observed? What if her choice would collapse not just her own wave function, but all of theirs?

Martin led them in meditation. Mitch caught more fish. Mark stared at the horizon with hollow eyes in between checking ship gauges that no longer turned.

And Montana felt the submarine drawing closer, rising through the dark water beneath them, bringing with it the end of this strange suspension, this quantum moment where all possibilities still existed simultaneously.

Soon, she would have to choose.

Soon, the wave function would collapse.

But not yet. Not tonight.

67

Tonight, they were still entangled, still coherent, still drifting in the space between what was and what would be.

Tonight, they were still Schrödinger's survivors—simultaneously saved and lost, alive and dying, together and alone, organization and entropy, if not consciousness and mechanicalistic manifestation.

The stars emerged overhead, distant and cold and beautiful, and Montana wondered if they too were entangled, if the light that reached her eyes had been traveling for so long that the stars themselves might already had ever existed at all.

She closed her eyes and felt Martin's consciousness beside her own, warm and bright and impossibly close.

And somewhere below, in the crushing darkness of the deep ocean, something vast and mechanical was rising to meet them.

Chapter Six: Surfacing

The ship existed in a state of quantum superposition—simultaneously sinking and saved, dying and living, lost and found. Montana stood at the rail in the pre-dawn darkness, practicing what some spiritual teachers called "self remembering": the deliberate division of attention between the observer and the observed, between the one who watches and the one who drifts. She felt the cold air on her skin. She noted her breathing. She attempted to be present to the moment rather than collapsing into the mechanical patterns of worry that had dominated her consciousness, especially since the storm.

Most humans, spirituality taught, live in sleep. They move through life as automatons, responding mechanically to stimuli, their essence buried beneath layers of personality—that false self. constructed of others. Montana had spent years in yoga classes trying to distinguish between these two aspects of herself: the essential Montana who painted mermaids in her Brooklyn studio, and the personality Montana who had fled her father's judgment, who had built walls of independence to protect a wounded core.

Now, drifting on a damaged vessel in the middle of the Pacific, surrounded by rescued animals whose collective body heat created a thermal signature that bloomed across the infrared spectrum like a small sun, she wondered if this entire voyage had been a form of conscious labor—that intentional effort toward awakening that teachers insisted on, was the only path to real being through suffering.

The animals slept in their makeshift pens and enclosures. The dogs huddled together.

The cats occupied every elevated surface. The birds had finally quieted. Even the horses had settled into an uneasy peace, assured that no human begrudged them their hay. Their combined presence transformed the ship into something unprecedented—a floating ark that registered on sonar, not as a small, damaged vessel, but as something massive, something that defied categorization.

simply stood beside her in what some teachings called the first conscious shock— that moment of voluntary attention that interrupts the mechanical flow of life. They had been through something together, these past hours. The storm,. The rescue. The impossible logistics of saving so many lives. It had stripped away personality and revealed essence.

"Martin's monitoring the radio," Mark said finally. "Nothing yet."

Montana nodded. She was practicing divided attention: aware of Mark's presence, aware of her own internal state, aware of the ship's gentle rocking, aware of the vast ocean that surrounded them. This was self-remembering— this simultaneous awareness of inner and outer, this refusal to be absorbed completely by any single phenomenon. To observe herself and Mark with a two-headed arrow. Without judgement and only with a wish for self-knowledge no matter with whom, where, or why.

"Do you think—" Mark began, yet stopped.

The ocean answered before he could finish.

It came from below, from the depths—a disturbance in the quantum field of probability that surrounded them. The water concentric circles. And then, with the inexorable force like something massive rising from the unconscious into consciousness, the submarine surfaced.

It came up directly beside them, so close that the displacement of water nearly capsized their already damaged vessel. The ship tilted violently. Animals cried out. Montana grabbed the rail as the deck pitched beneath her feet. The submarine's conning tower rose like a dark monument against the radiantly lightening dawn sky, water streaming from its surfaces, its hull painted with something that made Montana's heart stop.

A mermaid. A woman beneath the water.

Not just any mermaid, but *her* mermaid—
the one she had painted in her Brooklyn
studio six months earlier, working late into
the night, trying to capture something she
couldn't name. The figure she had created in
blues and greens and silvers, with eyes that
looked both human and other, with a tail that
seemed to dissolve into pure light at its
edges. She had painted it in a fever of
inspiration, feeling as though she were
channeling something rather than creating it,
as though the image already existed in some
Platonic realm and she was merely making it
visible.

And now here it was, rendered in marine
paint on the hull of a submarine that had
risen from the depths to save them.

This was what spiritual teachers sometimes
call a conscious shock from the universe—
those moments when the ordinary flow of
mechanical life is interrupted by something so
improbable, so precisely meaningful, that it
cannot be dismissed as coincidence. Montana
felt tears on her face. She was present to this

moment in a way she had not been present to anything in years.

"Montana," Mark whispered. "That's **_your_** painting."

She couldn't speak. The submarine settled in the water beside them, massive and impossible. Its hatch remained closed. Montana found herself suspended between two possibilities, two quantum states that had not yet collapsed into a single reality: Were the occupants mechanical devils or conscious angels? Had they come to save or to judge? Was this rescue or reckoning? Why did the energy suspended in the marine mist feel so terribly familiar? She almost expected family to appear before them.

The hatch opened.

A woman emerged first—not her mother, not her father, but someone else entirely. She was French, clearly, with that particular toughness that cannot be imitated. She wore coveralls that somehow looked chic, and her dark hair was pulled back in a practical bun that revealed a face of striking beauty. She moved with the confidence of someone who had designed this vessel, who understood every rivet and seal, who had bent metal and physics to her will.

"Bonjour," she called up to them, her voice carrying easily across the water. "I am Simone Archambault. We have been looking for you."

Then came the crew—four men in the uniforms of Castellan's foundation, moving with military precision to secure lines between the vessels. And then, finally, emerging into the dawn light like figures from Montana's unconscious made manifest, came . . . her parents.

Hugh Reeves first. Her father. Older now, his hair sprinkled with much more gray than she remembered, but still carrying himself with that same rigid certainty that had driven him hard in life and chased her away. The man who had told her not to come home if she got pregnant at just the age of 12! For no reason.

The man whose judgment had felt like a death sentence. He looked up at the damaged ship, his eyes scanning the deck until they found her.

He looked up at the damaged ship, his eyes scanning the deck until they found her.

Their gazes locked. Montana felt the collision of past and present, essence and personality, the wounded child and the woman she had become. This was intentional suffering—that voluntary acceptance of pain that gurus teach is necessary for growth. She could have looked away. She could have retreated into mechanical patterns of resentment and defense. Instead, she held his gaze and remained present to whatever was about to unfold.

Julian Reeves emerged behind her husband. Montana's mother. The Jungian psychologist who had always tried to bridge the gap between father and daughter, who had written papers about the collective unconscious while her own family fractured along fault lines of judgment and pride. She looked up at Montana with an expression that contained multitudes—relief, love, sorrow, hope.

"Montana," her mother called, her voice breaking slightly on the name.

The two vessels were secured together now. Simone Archambault was already climbing aboard the damaged ship with the grace of someone who had spent her life moving between sea and land, between the depths and the surface. She surveyed the animals with evident surprise, then turned to Mark straighten.

"You have been busy," she said. "This is quite the ark you have built. No?"

Mark, usually so articulate, seemed to have lost the capacity for speech. He managed something that might have been agreement.

Martin emerged from below deck, drawn by the commotion. When he saw Simone, something shifted in his expression— recognition of a kindred spirit, perhaps, or simply appreciation for someone who moved through the world with such evident competence. "You're the cockpit designer," he said.

"I am," Simone confirmed. "And you are the ones who have been broadcasting distress signals that make no sense. A ship that appears on sonar to be the size of a small island, with a heat signature that suggests either a floating hotel or a very confused whale."

"The animals emit a lot of heat," Martin explained.

"Ah." Simone's smile widened. "That explains much."

Montana's parents were climbing aboard now, her father moving stiffly, her mother reunion approached like a wave function about to collapse, like Schrödinger's box about to be opened. Montana stood at the rail, practicing self-remembering, trying to remain present rather than disappearing into mechanical reactions.

Her father reached the deck. He stood before her, this man who had shaped so much of her life through his absence and his judgment. For 30 seconds moment, neither spoke. Then Hugh Reeves did something Montana had never seen him do: he wept.

"I'm sorry," he said, his voice rough with emotion. "I'm so sorry, Montana. I was wrong. I was mechanical. I was asleep. I've been working—your mother got me into meditation and yoga—and I've been trying to wake up, to see life in the moment. In sleep, I have been reacting rather than responding, judging rather than loving."

Montana felt something crack open inside her—not breaking, but opening, like a seed splitting to allow sprouting. This was conscious labor, this meeting of essence to essence, stripped of the false personalities they had both worn for so long.

"Dad," she said, and found herself in his arms, both of them crying, both of them present to this moment of reconciliation that before had been impossible.

Julian Reeves waited, giving them space, her psychologist's training evident in her patience. When they finally separated, she embraced Montana with fierce intensity. "We've been tracking you," she said. "When Castellan told us about the voyage, about the animals, about everything—we had to come. We had to find you."

"The painting," Montana said, gesturing to the submarine. "How—"

"You sent me a photo of it," her mother said.

"Remember? Six months ago. I showed it to Simone when she was designing the submarine. She fell in love with it. Said it captured something essential about the relationship between consciousness and the depths."

Simone had been examining the ship's damage, but now she turned back to them. "It is a remarkable painting," she said to Montana. "It speaks of things that cannot be spoken. When your mother showed it to me, I knew it had to be on the hull. A submarine is a vessel that moves between worlds—

80

between air and water, between consciousness and the unconscious. Your mermaid understands this."

The sun was rising now, painting the sky in colors that seemed impossible—pinks and golds and purples that no mechanical process could produce. The animals were waking, their sounds creating a symphony of life that rose from the damaged ship like a prayer or chanting.

"We should celebrate," Simone announced suddenly. "We have found each other." She glanced at Mark. "We are alive. The universe has brought us together in a way that defies probability. This deserves acknowledgment."

"I have wine," one of Castellan's crew members offered. "In the submarine. For emergencies."

Mark mumbled something about definition of "emergency" and then coming to his senses, smiled at Simone.

"This qualifies," Simone said decisively.

As the wine was retrieved and poured into whatever containers could be found, Simone began to sing. Her voice was extraordinary—rich and full, carrying across the water with the kind of beauty that stops time. She sang something in French, something old and haunting, about the sea and love and the eternal return.

Martin, who had been standing slightly apart, suddenly joined her. His voice blended with that was more than the sum of its parts. They sang together as the sun rose, as the two vessels rocked gently in the swells, as the animals listened with what seemed like conscious attention.

Montana stood between her parents, Mark beside her, watching Martin and Simone create beauty from sound and breath and intention. This was what some teachers call a higher center moment—when the intellectual and emotional centers align with something beyond ordinary consciousness, when the mechanical gives way to the essential, when sleep transforms into waking.

The ship was still damaged. They were still adrift. The journey was far from over. But they were no longer alone, no longer lost. They had surfaced— literally and metaphorically—into a new configuration of possibility.

Montana looked at the mermaid painted on the submarine's hull, seeing her own creation, reflected back to her from the depths, and understood that she had been painting a prophecy. The mermaid was herself—caught between worlds, learning to breathe in both air and water, learning to navigate the boundary between consciousness and the unconscious, between essence and personality, between the mechanical life she had fled and the conscious life she was learning to inhabit.

"To surfacing," her father said, raising his cup.

"To waking up," her mother added.

"To conscious labor," Montana said, and they drank together as the sun rose and the sea

held them all in its vast, objective, perfect
embrace.

Chapter Seven: Mars Rising

The golden sun cast long shadows across the reconstructed Superlative facility at dawn. Its gleaming steel and glass architecture rising from the New Mexico desert like a phoenix reborn. Twenty-six years had passed since the storm that had nearly destroyed everything, and now, in the spring of 2027, the compound stood as a testament to human resilience and vision. The main building stretched across fifteen acres, its curved walls designed to mimic the aerodynamics of spacecraft, while solar panels glittered like scales across every available surface.

Montana stood at the observation deck of the central tower, her auburn hair now lightly streaked with distinguished threads of silver, her green eyes still as penetrating as they had been in her youth. At forty-seven she carried herself with the grace of someone who had learned to balance ambition with wisdom, passion with patience, artistry with science. Below her, the facility hummed with purposeful activity as scientists, veterinarians, and engineers moved between sunlight like wings. Still amazing to have mostly the same, well paid, team, only a few of whom had moved on. Montana, Mitch, Martin, and Mark had all remained married to their jobs.

The press conference had concluded an hour ago, and already the news was spreading across every media platform on Earth. After decades of secrecy, the Superlative Dawn mission had finally been revealed to the world. The technology they had perfected—true artificial weightlessness, not the crude simulation of parabolic flights or the expensive reality of orbital stations, but genuine gravitational manipulation—had been demonstrated to a stunned audience of journalists, scientists, and government officials. The heightened conscious awareness that seemed to also flourish in their experiments remained hidden except to those who had found their way to understanding the experience on their own.

Montana had watched from the balcony as Mitch Henderson, now Chief Operations Officer of the facility, had explained the breakthrough with the calm authority of someone who had earned his position through years of dedication and sacrifice. His dark hair was peppered with gray now, and the lines around his eyes spoke of sleepless nights and impossible decisions, but there was something else in his bearing—a quiet confidence that hadn't been there before, a depth that suggested he had traveled to places most people never glimpsed and returned transformed.

She had noticed, over the past few months, how seamlessly she and Mitch worked together. Where once there had been friction and misunderstanding, now there was an almost telepathic harmony. He would anticipate her needs before she voiced them. She would understand his concerns before he raised them. It was as if some invisible

87

barrier between them had dissolved, leaving only a clear channel of communication that transcended words.

"Quite a day," Martin's voice came from behind her, and she turned to find her mentor standing in the doorway, his white hair luminous in the morning light. At sixty-nine, Martin Crawls moved with the careful deliberation of age, but his deep Earth brown eyes remained sharp, missing nothing. "The world finally knows what we've been building."

"It feels strange," Montana admitted, turning back to the window. "After all these years of secrecy, to have it out in the open."

The technicians stepped back, and the chamber's systems engaged with a low hum that Montana could feel in her bones. The air itself seemed to shimmer, as if reality were adjusting its parameters. And then, slowly, impossibly, Galileo began to rise.

The horse's hooves lifted from the ground, first the front, then the back, until he hung suspended in the center of the chamber like a living sculpture. Three feet. Ten feet. Fifteen feet off the ground. For a moment, he thrashed, instinct overriding training, but then his handlers' voices reached him—calm, reassuring—and he stilled. His legs extended gracefully, his mane floating around his neck like a halo, his dark eyes wide but unafraid.

Montana felt tears sear her eyes with wonder and gratitude. This was what they had been working toward all these years—not just the technology, but the trust, the relationship between human and animal that made such a thing possible. Galileo hung in the air for a full minute, turning slowly in the invisible currents of manipulated gravity, before the technicians gently lowered him back to the ground. The horse landed with perfect balance, shook his mane, and whinnied as if to say, "Is that all?"

"Beautiful," Montana whispered. "Everything is ready," Martin said. "The ship, the animals, the technology. All that remains is the final selection."

Montana knew what he meant. The Mars mission would launch in six months, and while she would lead the animal research component, she needed a second-in command—someone who could handle both the technical demands and the unpredictable challenges of deep space travel with living creatures. Someone she could trust with her life and the lives of the animals in her care.

Three applications sat on her desk in the office below. Three men, each qualified in different ways, each representing a different possible future.

Mark Rubin had been the first to apply. Now fifty-five, he had spent the past two decades building his reputation as one of the world's leading experts in space vehicle architecture. His research on metal density in zero gravity had revolutionized the field. He was brilliant, dedicated, and still carried a torch for Montana that he had never quite managed to extinguish, despite his on-again, off-again relationship with Simone Archambeau, who had become the facility's chief space capsule designer.

Martin, himself, had submitted an application, though Montana suspected it was more symbolic than sincere. At his age, the rigors of space travel would be challenging, but he had argued that his experience and intuitive understanding of animal behavior made him uniquely qualified. Montana knew the real reason— Martin had always been a teacher, and he couldn't resist the opportunity to guide her through one more transformation.

And then there was Mitch.

His application had been the last to arrive, and the most surprising. Mitch had never expressed interest in space travel before. His domain was operations, logistics, the practical realities of keeping a complex facility running smoothly. But his letter had been compelling, speaking of unfinished Montana's were meant to converge in ways neither of them had yet fully explored.

There was something else, too—something Montana had only recently learned. During the rescue operation after the storm twenty-six years before, Mitch had been knocked unconscious by the *Superlative* and submarine collision and had been clinically dead for nearly four minutes. The submarine paramedic had revived him, but he had never spoken publicly about what he had experienced during those minutes. Only now, in his application letter, had he mentioned it: a journey through darkness into light, a sense of connection to something vast and incomprehensible, and a vision of Montana standing on red soil beneath a pink sky, calling his name.

A near-death experience. Montana had read enough about such phenomena to know they often changed people in fundamental ways, opening doors of perception that had previously been closed. Was that what she had been sensing in Mitch these past months? Had his brush with death awakened something in him, some latent capacity that now resonated with her own developing abilities?

92

She thought of the quantum entanglement Martin had taught her about—how two particles, once connected, remained linked across any distance, each affecting the other instantaneously. Was that what was happening between her and Mitch? Had the storm, the near-death, the years of working in parallel created some kind of entanglement between their shared beings?

"You already know who you're going to choose," Martin said, reading her thoughts as he so often did.

"Do I?" Montana asked, though she knew he was right.

"The heart knows before the mind accepts," Martin said. "But sometimes the mind needs a little push."

That night, Montana worked late in her office, reviewing mission protocols and animal transport specifications. The facility was quiet, most of the staff having gone home hours ago. Only the night shift remained, their footsteps echoing occasionally in the distant corridors.

At three in the morning, exhausted and unable to focus any longer, Montana finally closed her laptop and leaned back in her chair. She closed her eyes, intending to rest for just a moment, but instead found herself slipping into that liminal space between waking and sleeping, where the boundaries become merely improbable.

In that space, she felt Martin's presence—not physically, but as a distinct consciousness touching her own. And then, like a gift placed gently in her hands, came a vision.

She saw herself and Mitch walking together across red sand, the sun setting behind them casting their shadows long and intertwined. They were holding hands, moving in perfect synchronization, their steps matching as if choreographed by some cosmic intelligence. The sky above them was the dusty pink of

Mars at dusk, and in the distance, the Superlative Dawn habitat domes glowed like pearls against the alien landscape.

But it was the feeling that accompanied the vision that struck Montana most powerfully—

a sense of rightness, of completion, of two paths that had been running parallel finally converging into one. This was not Martin showing her what should be, but what already was, in some dimension of reality that existed beyond linear time.

Montana's eyes snapped open, her heart racing. The vision faded, but its emotional resonance remained, thrumming through her like a plucked string. She looked at the clock: 3:17 a.m. Somewhere in the facility, she knew, Martin was awake, having just sense of his own being.

She picked up her phone and typed an invitation to the three applicants in separate messages: "Please meet me in the meditation chamber tomorrow at 8 p.m. Come alone."

The meditation chamber had been Montana's design, authorized by the founder, Mr. Castellan, a circular room at the heart of the facility where she went to center herself before important decisions. The floor was a circular covered indoor pool, its surface hidden beneath a specialized membrane that could support weight but also spin and move in response to the room's environmental controls. Around the perimeter, in spacious and luxuriously appointed enclosures, lived some of the animals selected for the Mars mission: a pair of rabbits, three chickens, two cats, and a small dog named Cosmo who had been training in the weightlessness chamber for two years.

Montana arrived early, wanting time to prepare herself. She wore simple clothes—jeans and a white eyelet shirt—and had pulled her hair back in a loose braid. The animals stirred as she entered, recognizing her presence, and she moved around the room greeting each one, her hands gentle on reassuring.

Finally, she moved to the center of the room, to the circular platform that rose slightly above the pool cover. She sat cross-legged, closed her eyes, and began to observe her breathing, centering herself in the present moment.

She heard them arrive, one by one. First Mark, entering through the east doorway, his footsteps confident and familiar. Then Martin, from the north, moving more slowly but with deliberate purpose. And finally, Mitch, from the west, his presence somehow more substantial than the others, as if he carried more weight in the fabric of reality itself.

Montana kept her eyes closed, aware of them standing in their respective doorways, waiting. The air in the room felt charged, electric with possibility and tension.

And then, without warning, the pool cover began to spin.

Montana's eyes flew open. The membrane beneath her was rotating slowly, like a record on a turntable, and she had to adjust her balance to remain centered. The animals around the perimeter began to stir, sensing the change in the room's energy.

three men, one in each door, silhouetted against the light from the corridors beyond. Mark and Martin stood with their hands slightly raised, their faces intense with

97

concentration, and Montana realized with a shock that they were doing this—somehow, by telekinesis, through force of will or psychic ability or some combination of both, they were manipulating the pool cover's rotation.

It was a test, she understood. A demonstration. They were showing her their capabilities, their power, their worthiness.

The cover spun faster, and Montana had to focus to maintain her balance. The animals were becoming agitated now, the rabbits thumping in their enclosure, the chickens clucking nervously, Cosmo barking sharp warnings.

"Stop," Montana called out, but the spinning continued, accelerating.

She looked toward Mitch, and what she saw in his face was different from the other two.

He wasn't concentrating or straining. Instead, he looked concerned, focused not on demonstrating power but on her safety. And as their eyes met across the spinning room, something passed between them— a understanding.

Mitch's expression changed, becoming very still, very centered. He didn't raise his hands or make any dramatic gesture. He simply stood there, sensing his spine, and Montana felt something shift in the room's energy. The spinning began to slow. The water beneath the membrane seemed to calm, as if responding to some unspoken command.

It was Mitch. Somehow, in that moment, he had discovered an ability he hadn't known he possessed—the power not to control or manipulate, but to soothe, to calm, to bring peace to chaos.

The pool cover stopped spinning entirely, settling into perfect stillness. The animals quieted, sensing the return of equilibrium.

And then the lights went out.

In the sudden darkness, Montana heard Mark's voice, sharp with authority: "Emergency protocols! Everyone, stay calm!" And Martin's voice, equally commanding:

99

"Staff to stations! Secure the animals!"

But Montana wasn't listening to them. In the darkness, she felt rather than saw Mitch move. There was a click, and a beam of light cut through the blackness—Mitch's flashlight, prepared.

He moved toward her, the light steady in his hand, and Montana stood. The pool cover was finally standing still beneath her feet, but she knew it was also treacherous, that one wrong step could send her plunging into the water below.

"Montana," Mitch's voice came through the darkness, calm and sure. "Walk toward me. I've got you."

She took a step, then another, her arms extended for balance. The beam of his flashlight guided her, and she focused on it like a beacon, trusting that he would lead her true.

Behind her, she could hear Mark and Martin still calling out instructions, trying to manage the situation, but their voices seemed to fade into background noise. All that mattered was the light ahead and the man holding it.

Montana reached the edge of the pool cover, and Mitch's hand extended toward her. She took it, feeling the warmth and strength of his grip, and he pulled her safely onto solid ground.

For a moment, they stood For a moment, they stood there in the darkness, hands clasped, the flashlight beam pointing downward and casting their shadows long against the walls. Montana could feel her heart pounding, could hear Mitch's breathing, could sense the electricity that had always existed between them finally finding its proper circuit.

"There's another door," Mitch said softly, and Montana realized he was right. In the chaos and darkness, she had forgotten about the south entrance—the one that led to the observation deck overlooking the launch facility.

Still holding hands, they moved toward it, leaving Mark and Martin behind in the darkness. The door opened silently, and they stepped through into a corridor bathed in emergency lighting. But it was what lay beyond the corridor's windows that made Montana gasp.

The observation deck opened onto a view of the night sky, and there, hanging low on the horizon like a promise, was Mars. The red planet gleamed against the darkness, brighter than she had ever seen it, as if it were calling to them, beckoning them forward into their shared destiny.

Mitch turned to her, and in the dim light, Montana could see everything she needed to know written in his face—the years of patience, the quiet devotion, the journey he wisdom he had gained along the way.

"I died once," he said quietly. "And when I came back, I saw you. On Mars. Waiting for me. I didn't understand it then, but I do now."

Montana felt tears streaming down her face, years of resistance and fear and uncertainty finally dissolving. "I've been so blind," she whispered.

"No," Mitch said, reaching up to gently wipe away her tears. "You've been on your own journey. We both have. But now . . ...." "Now our paths converge," Montana finished.

He smiled, and it transformed his face, making him look younger, lighter, as if some burden he had been carrying for decades had finally been lifted. "Now our paths converge," he agreed.

Montana rose on her toes, and Mitch bent his head, and their lips met in a kiss that felt like coming home after a long journey through foreign lands. It was gentle and fierce, tentative and certain, a first kiss and a thousandth kiss all at once.

When they gracefully pulled apart, Mars still hung in the window behind them, patient would dare to make it their home.

The next morning, Montana made her announcement. Mitch Henderson would accompany her to Mars as second-in command of the animal research mission. The decision surprised no one who had been paying attention, though it raised a few eyebrows among those who hadn't noticed the shift in dynamics between the two.

Mark Rubin took the news with grace, though Montana could see the flicker of disappointment in his eyes. But that disappointment was tempered by something else—relief, perhaps, or recognition that he had been pursuing the wrong dream for the wrong reasons.

Two days later, Montana found Mark and Simone in the facility's garden, sitting close together on a bench beneath a flowering jacaranda tree. They were holding hands, their heads bent together in intimate conversation, and Montana felt a surge of happiness for them both. Mark had spent so many years chasing a fantasy of what he thought he wanted that he had nearly missed the reality of what he needed. Simone, with her creative design insight and out.

Martin's reaction to Montana's decision was characteristically enigmatic. He simply smiled and nodded, as if he had known all along how things would unfold. "The universe has a way of arranging itself," he said. "We just have to be wise enough to recognize the pattern."

A week after the announcement, Martin came to Montana's office with news of his own. He would be leaving the Superlative Dawn facility, he told her, to join a research expedition with the Dalai Lama's team, studying the intersection of consciousness and quantum mechanics in the Himalayan monasteries' music.

"It's time," he said simply. "I've taught you everything I can. The rest of your journey is yours to make."

Montana felt a pang of loss, but also a sense of rightness. Martin had been her teacher, her guide, her ethereal spiritual lover, and her mentor for so many years, but she was no longer the uncertain young woman who had first arrived at the facility. She had grown into her own power, her own wisdom, her own understanding.

Will you come back?" she asked.

"Perhaps," Martin said. "But not before you return from Mars. Some journeys must be made alone—or in your case, with the right companion."

He glanced meaningfully toward the window, where Mitch could be seen crossing the courtyard below, and Montana smiled.

"Mark and Simone will accompany me," Martin continued. "Mark's expertise will be valuable in studying the effects of sound moving though architecture on consciousness, and Simone's vocal training will help us understand what we discover and how to adjust acoustics. We'll be a good team."

Montana hugged him then as if it should last forever. This man who had shaped so much of her life, who had seen potential in her when she couldn't see it herself, who had pushed and challenged and supported her through every transformation.

"Thank you," she whispered. "For everything."

"Thank you," Martin replied, "for having the courage to become who you were meant to be."

The months before launch passed in a blur of final preparations and training. Montana and Mitch worked side by side, their partnership deepening with each passing day. They learned each other's rhythms, each other's strengths and weaknesses, each other's fears and hopes.

At night, they would stand on the observation deck, watching Mars rise, planning their future on that distant world. They talked about the habitat they would build, the research they would conduct, the animals they would care for. But they also talked about simpler things—what they would miss about Earth, what they hoped to discover about themselves, how strange and wonderful it was to have finally found each other after so many years of circling in separate orbits.

Montana sighed. "It only took simplifying travel to Mars into a four year trip to help me find true love."

"Do you ever wonder," Mitch asked one night, "if the storm was meant to happen? If I was meant to die and come back, just so I could be ready for this?"

Montana considered the question. "I don't know if anything is 'meant' to happen," she said slowly. "But I think sometimes the universe presents us with opportunities to transform, and it's up to us whether we take them. You could have come back from that experience closed off and traumatized. Instead, you let it open you up."

"I had a good reason to stay open," Mitch said, pulling her close. "Even if I didn't fully understand it at the time."

Three nights before Martin, Mark, and Simone were to leave for India, the five of them gathered for a final dinner in Montana's quarters. They ate simply—pasta and salad and good wine—and talked late into the night about everything and nothing.

Mark and Simone sat close together, their body language speaking of a relationship that had finally found its proper foundation. They would spend a year in India with Martin, they explained, and then return to establish a new research center focused on consciousness studies in tiny home building. They were excited, energized, ready for their own adventure after building the vehicle Mitch and Montana would travel in.

Martin was even quieter than usual, but his eyes were bright with anticipation. At sixty-seven, he was embarking on what might be his final great journey, and he approached it with the enthusiasm of a much younger man.

"To new beginnings," Montana said, raising her glass.

"To convergence," Martin added.

"To love," Simone said, smiling at Mark.

109

"To courage," Mark offered.

"To coming home," Mitch finished, looking at Montana.

They clinked glasses, and in that moment, Montana felt the rightness of it all—the way their paths had woven together and apart and together again, creating a pattern that was more beautiful for its complexity.

Launch day dawned clear and bright, the New Mexico sky a perfect blue dome overhead. The Superlative Dawn spacecraft stood on its pad like a silver needle pointing toward the heavens, ready to carry its precious cargo across the vast darkness between worlds.

Montana and Mitch stood in the crew quarters, helping each other with the final checks on their flight suits. The animals were already aboard, secured in their specially designed habitats, calm and trusting after years of training. "Ready?" Mitch asked, and Montana nodded.

They walked together through the facility one last time, saying goodbye to the place that had been home for so many years. The staff lined the corridors, applauding as they passed, and Montana felt her throat tighten with emotion.

At the entrance to the launch tower, they found Martin, Mark, and Simone waiting. Martin stepped forward and embraced Montana one final time.

"Remember," he said softly, "the greatest discoveries are not made in outer space, but in inner space. Mars will teach you things about yourself you never imagined.

... I will always be with you."

"I'll remember," Montana promised.

Mark hugged her next, and there was no awkwardness in it, only genuine affection and friendship. "Take care of each other," he said.

"We will," Montana replied.

Simone's embrace was warm and sisterly. "I always knew you two would end up together,"

111

she whispered. "I'm glad you finally figured it out."

Then Mitch was shaking hands with the three of them, receiving their blessings and good wishes, and then it was time to go.

Montana and Mitch entered the elevator that would carry them up the launch tower. As the doors closed, Montana caught one last glimpse of Martin, Mark, and Simone standing together, waving. Then the elevator began to rise, and they were gone.

At the top of the tower, they crossed the gangway into the spacecraft. The interior was sleek and functional, every surface designed for maximum efficiency. But there were touches of warmth too—photographs of Earth, plants growing in hydroponic gardens, and in the animal research section, the familiar faces of their charges waiting patiently for the journey to begin.

Montana moved through the animal habitats, checking on each creature one final time. Galileo, the Arabian stallion who had floated so gracefully in the demonstration, whinnied softly as she approached. She stroked his nose, whispering reassurances.

"We're going on an adventure, beautiful boy," she said. "The greatest outer adventure of all."

In the cockpit, Mitch was running through the pre-flight checklist with the pilot and navigator. Montana joined him, strapping into her seat, feeling the familiar mixture of excitement and terror that came before any great leap into the unknown.

It was a new beginning. It was a convergence of paths. It was the fulfillment of dreams that had been two decades in the making.

And as the Superlative Dawn disappeared into the vast darkness between worlds, carrying Montana and Mitch and their animal companions toward Mars, one thing was to be certain: whatever challenges lay ahead, whatever discoveries awaited them, whatever transformations they would undergo in that alien landscape, they would face it all together, energy and mass. The Superlative Dawn would sail on through the darkness, carrying its precious cargo of hope and life and love toward the future, while behind it, the Earth grew smaller, and smaller, until it was just another star in the infinite tapestry of the cosmos. It moved from one earthbound scale to another containing the entire galaxy.

The countdown began, and Mitch reached for Montana's hand. Mitch was grinning, his face alight with joy and wonder. She accepted his grip, strong and steady, and they sat together in silence as the numbers ticked down toward zero, ready to paint the next chapter of their story on the blank canvas of section, Nebula, the horse, dreamed of running across red plains beneath a renewed sun, his hooves kicking up dust that had never known the touch of Earth. And around him, the other creatures slept peacefully, trusting in the humans who had promised to keep them safe on this impossible journey. Behind them, would be Earth continuing its ancient dance around the sun, the absolute of our human scale. Somewhere on its surface, Martin, Mark, and Simone would be beginning their own adventures, following their own paths toward wisdom and love and understanding.

Ten. Nine. Eight.

Montana thought of all the years that had led to this moment—the storms weathered, the lessons learned, the transformations undergone.

Seven. Six. Five.

She thought of Mark and Simone, finally finding in each other what they had been seeking all along. She thought of Martin, mountains of India, seeking wisdom in ancient traditions. And felt her other hand squeezed as if he was there . . . . .

Four. Three. Two.

Montana and Mitch broke through the cloud layer, and suddenly the sky darkened from blue to black, and the stars came out, brilliant and unwavering. Earth fell away beneath them. That beautiful blue marble that had been home to every human who had ever lived, becoming just one world among many. The story that had begun with a storm and a near-death and a young woman's desperate dream had become something far greater than any of them could have imagined—a testament to the power of perseverance, the wisdom of patience, and the transformative force of love in a singularity.

One.

And the future, as always, was full of infinite possibility.

Deni Rodgers finished 11/27/2025

Deni Rodgers discovered art and literature in childhood and continues to pursue exploration and touch in the world, visually and poetically. She first published: an  essay, nationally, in 7th grade. She attended San Francisco Art Institute in the 70's, after studying Psychology at Colorado College, when it was 200 years old, where she invented her own version of art therapy. She has meditated for 40 years.

In 1973 the author painted "My Reflection in a Snow-Covered Hill", which honestly foretold events, people, relationships, and surprises for several years to come. It choreographed colliding past and future "characters" interfacing with each other almost in an animated fashion. (Honors to Fleetwood Mac) (Forthcoming is "Painting from Within" with illustrations. Methods to paint the unconscious.s)

At present she ranges from pure realism to fantasy to painting from the collective unconscious, as her starting points. She has shown in New York, San Francisco, Denver, Washington D.C. and Cern, Switzerland.

She has sung in Paris, France, Colorado and Newport, RI, USA.

Artist/Author statement:

Fantasies intertwining realism and dream are the objective of her art, creating images in a string of connections that make sense or open up questions. These images can lead to healing, inventions, and even insight into the future, where the conscious enters the viewers' unconscious and then, hopefully, eventually, the collective. It is as if her contemporary artistic process encourages the canvas to speak and the form of the symbol need not be well-defined and in fact may take several passes before it emerges enough to find its voice or reach the audience.

It can be said that both Van Gogh, with the turbulence of physics, and Pollock, with splatter meets-paint-by-number mirages, were, "acted upon" by inner forces, as were many in the movements of Surrealism and Abstract Expressionism. Picasso painted cubism just before the splitting of the atom. Deni is seeking to define her position as a translator of realism to deep unconscious portraiture, landscapes, and journalism within which the viewer plays a part in the choreography of seeing something new in the collective imagination of humanity.

www.ingramcontent.com/pod-product-compliance
Lightning Source LLC
Chambersburg PA
CBHW020252150626
46552CB00020B/778